Big Brave Brother Ben

STORY BY **KARA MAY**

PICTURES BY **GUS CLARKE**

Lothrop, Lee & Shepard Books   New York

Riley   Happy Valentines Day
        Love

        Grammy & Grampy

        1997

This is my big brother and his name is Ben.
My Big Brother Ben is ever so brave.
"I'm ever so brave!" says Ben.

"I slide from the top of the tallest slide.
I swing on the swing right up to the sky!
I'm ever so brave!" says Ben.

"What are you scared of, Ben?" ask I.
"Nothing!" he says.
"Not even spiders?"
"Who? Me?" says Ben.

"I'd let a tarantula sit on my head! In fact,
I'd let a whole family sleep in my bed.

I'm not scared of bats...

...and I'd sit in a cage with hundreds of rats!
I'm ever so brave!" says Ben.

I have a little think. And then I say, "If I was in the jungle and I met a tiger, I'd be scared stiff. Wouldn't you?"

"Listen," says Ben. "If *I* met a tiger in the middle of the jungle...

...I'd jump on his back and go for a ride!

And if I met a python...

...I'd climb him like a tree!

And if I met a crocodile...

I'd clean his teeth, every single one!
I'm ever so brave!" says Ben.

As we go home...

Ben punches at the air. "If I see a robber, this is what he'll get!"

WHAM!

THUMP!

THWACK!

"And if I see a monster from outer space...

...I'll pick him up with one hand, and send him whizzing home again! I'm ever so brave!" says Ben.

"Mum," say I, "Ben's ready for his tea."

All of a sudden, a question pops into my mind. "Ben," ask I, "are you frightened of the dark?"

Up jumps Ben...

...and switches off the light!
"I'm not frightened of the dark. I LOVE the
dark!" he says. "I'd go to a haunted castle...

...in the middle of the night, ALL BY MYSELF,
when the moon is full!

I'd walk through the spooks...

...and dance with Old Rattlebones.

I'd make spells with the wizards...

...and go flying with the witches.

And now," says Ben, "I've got a question for *you:* If a vampire walked in, would your hair stand on end? Would you scream? Would you faint?"
"I would!" say I.

"I wouldn't!" says Ben. "I'd shake him by the hand and ask him in for tea! Vampires drink blood but they don't scare me! I'm ever so brave! I'm INCREDIBLY brave!"

His tummy gives another rumble.
"And I'm ever so hungry. Mum!" he yells.
"What's happened to my tea?"

Now I'll tell you something else about
my Big Brave Brother Ben...

He's not scared of:

slides
swings
spiders
rats
bats
tigers
snakes
crocodiles
robbers
monsters
spooks
skeletons
witches
wizards
or
even
vampires

BUT
the funny thing is...
he's scared of ME!

when all I say is...